In the Rue Bel Tesoro

Written by Lin Coghlan

Illustrated by Philip Bannister

CHARACTERS

Omar

Sasha

Fran

Georgiou

Lena

Bruno

Norma

Fortune Teller

Soldier

IN THE RUE BEL TESORO

(The action of the play unfolds over 24 hours on the streets of a country in chaos.)

SCENE 1

(A busy train station crowded with travellers. Sasha and Omar arrive pushing an old-fashioned pram and carrying a bag stuffed with belongings.)

SASHA: Don't say anything, Omar, let me do the talking.

OMAR: *(into the pram)* You've got to keep quiet, Valentine, we're in the station now.

(Sasha and Omar approach a soldier checking documents at the entrance to the platform.)

SOLDIER: Papers?

SASHA: *(handing over the papers)* We're going to meet our mother. She's waiting for us.

SOLDIER: The baby – his pass?

SASHA: He's … a new baby, he doesn't have one.

OMAR: He's very new.

(Sasha glares at Omar.)

SOLDIER: No papers, I can't let you through.

(Fran arrives with a huge suitcase and pushes in.)

FRAN: Please – let an old woman by! My bad hip! My feet! (looking up at the soldier) Don't I know you? Why – of course, I used to knit with your mother, we baked bread together …

SOLDIER: *(unmoved)* Papers?

(Fran gives him her papers as the children watch.)

SOLDIER: Go through.

(Fran hurries through the barrier. Sasha grabs Omar and drags him after Fran, getting away from the soldier.)

SOLDIER: Hey you! Come back!

(Sasha and Omar disappear into the crowd.)

SCENE 2

(Sasha and Omar enter the train compartment.)

OMAR: We don't have any tickets. Mummy would be cross.

SASHA: Mummy would understand, we haven't enough money to buy tickets.

OMAR: But it's wrong not to pay.

SASHA: When we get to the city we'll send the train company the money and it'll be all right.

(Fran staggers into the compartment with her bundles.)

FRAN: Move! Out of my way! Oh, a baby! I hate babies. I'm afraid you'll have to go, I really can't travel with a baby.

SASHA: Please, madam, if we could stay with you, we're on our own …

FRAN: Oh no – impossible, I must have my space.

(She starts to get her things out: an old radio, a framed photograph of a dog. Omar picks up the photograph and looks at it.)

FRAN: Put that down!

(Omar puts it down.)

SASHA: It's easier to travel as a family.

FRAN: Not for me. Oh no.

SASHA: The soldiers don't stop old people so much when they have children.

FRAN: I don't like babies.

OMAR: It isn't a baby – it's a dog.

(Sasha looks at him furiously.)

OMAR: They were going to poison all the animals so we wrapped Valentine in a blanket and told him not to wag his tail.

FRAN: *(staring into the pram)* I had a dog when I was your age. A wonderful dog. I must have something to eat, it's past my teatime. What have you got to eat?

SASHA: We have bread and cheese.

FRAN: *(sniffs)* Yellow cheese, ummmm. I'll take some.

(Sasha gives Fran a piece of cheese. Fran offers the children nothing. Omar is poking about in the luggage. A big case falls down with a crash and opens on the floor. Dozens of sets of false teeth fall out on the floor.)

FRAN: What are you doing! Be careful! My business! Let children near you and this is what happens.

OMAR: Are all these teeth yours?

FRAN: No, no. Really! These teeth are my business. People will always need teeth. To eat, to whistle with, ever tried to whistle without your teeth?

OMAR: I can't whistle …

FRAN: Well, one day you will, and take it from me, no teeth, no whistling. *(to Sasha)* You want to get married? Eh? A girl needs her teeth. A woman will always survive as long as she has her business. We make our own luck in this life, there are no free rides.

(Fran climbs on to the top bunk, Omar and Sasha sit together on the bottom bunk, and the dog is in a bundle of blankets on top of them.)

FRAN: When we arrive in the morning I don't want you hanging around me, you hear? Asking for food and help. I have nothing for you, understand?

SASHA: Yes, madam.

FRAN: Quiet now, I must rest. *(starting to sing softly to herself)*

> Lay you down in the starry night …
> Moon above you shining bright
> Papa comes with meat and bread
> Mama rocks you in your bed
> Soon you'll wake to golden sun …
> Sleep in peace the day is done.

OMAR: *(to Sasha)* Remember when Mummy used to sing that? Have you got the letter? With Auntie's address?

SASHA: How many times are you going to ask me?

OMAR: Can I hold it?

(Sasha hands him a crumpled piece of paper.)

OMAR: Valentine, look, this is the paper with Auntie's address. That's where we're going. Everything will be all right. Isn't that right, Sasha?

SASHA: Shush, Omar, go to sleep.

(The train travels on through the night.)

SCENE 3

(It's morning. Sasha and Omar stand with the pram and their bag facing Fran.)

FRAN: Goodbye.

SASHA: Perhaps we might travel with you?

FRAN: I'm not going your way. Too bad. Must get on, I have appointments, goodbye.

(Fran leaves. Sasha and Omar stand there unsure of what to do.)

SASHA: Maybe there's a bus. Stay there and don't talk to anyone. What did I say?

OMAR: Don't talk to anyone.

(Sasha goes. Omar stands with the pram. Georgiou and Lena arrive. Georgiou takes out a little folding table and sets it up, with some objects under a cloth. Lena gets out a hat.)

GEORGIOU: Ladies and gentlemen, come closer, I have many miracles to show you, mysteries.

(Omar stares at him.)

GEORGIOU: Sir, for a few pennies, an apple fully grown inside a bottle … I put it there myself, ask me how.

(No one is interested.)

GEORGIOU: Madam, the hair of a mermaid, to bring you luck. Just to wish on it is good for you … My sister will be passing amongst you with a hat, whatever you give we are grateful, we are alone and depend on your kindness.

(Sasha returns.)

SASHA: All the buses are full. We'll have to walk.

(Lena hands Georgiou the hat and he takes a few coins out of it. Sasha and Omar watch him take the money. Lena stares into the pram.)

LENA: You've got a doggie in a pram.

GEORGIOU: Come on, Lena, we're going.

(Georgiou and Lena turn to go.)

SASHA: *(stopping them)* Do you know which way, to the city?

GEORGIOU: There are lots of ways, but it's hard to get through, roadblocks, barricades.

SASHA: We have dried fruit.

(Georgiou glances over.)

SASHA: We don't ask any favours.
We'll give you some dates in payment,
and you'll take us where we need to go.

(Georgiou puts his hand out for payment.)

SASHA: After.

(Georgiou nods. The children start walking.)

OMAR: How did you get the apple inside the bottle?

GEORGIOU: When you've been with the fair for 20 years, then I can tell you.

OMAR: But you're not that old.

GEORGIOU: No. But my father is a fairman, and I've got the secrets in my bones.

(They walk off.)

SCENE 4

(Fran sits opposite a Fortune Teller in a caravan. A parrot sits preening itself. The Fortune Teller shakes a bag full of shells and throws them across the table. Fran stares eagerly at the pattern they make.)

FRAN: What do the shells say?

FORTUNE TELLER: You've experienced an act of kindness.

FRAN: Nonsense! When?

FORTUNE TELLER: A treasure has been within your grasp … but you let it slip from your fingers.

FRAN: A treasure? Silver? Gold? I saw nothing.

FORTUNE TELLER: I say only what I see.

FRAN: Where is the usual fortune teller? I want the one I always see …

FORTUNE TELLER: *(clearing away)* My wife and children left for the city ten days ago – we needed rations. I thought they'd attract less attention travelling alone.

FRAN: There's not a loaf of bread or a piece of meat to be found, it's true.

FORTUNE TELLER: *(sadly)* I expected them back by now. I should never have let them go.

FRAN: Here's money for you but you're not much of a fortune teller – a treasure indeed!

(Fran leaves.)

FORTUNE TELLER: *(to the parrot)* Lucky, go tell the horses to finish their food, we're leaving within the hour.

(sound effect: a parrot's squawk)

SCENE 5

(It's evening in a church bell tower. Georgiou is unpacking. Lena's sitting on a blanket setting out her toys. Sasha and Omar climb up the wooden steps.)

GEORGIOU: I told you to find your own place.

SASHA: We don't know anywhere.

(Georgiou keeps unpacking.)

SASHA: We have some cheese left.

(Georgiou puts his hand out. Sasha pays him with a piece of cheese. Georgiou lays out a line of bottles each containing fully grown fruit.)

OMAR: Look, Sasha, a big apple in a bottle.

LENA: We can't eat them because they make us money.

SASHA: How do you get them inside?

OMAR: You have to be with the fair for 20 years before you can know.

LENA: Are you all on your own?

OMAR: Our mother had to go and answer questions when the soldiers came.

LENA: We were buying olive oil in a shop but then there was shooting and our mummy said, "Run," so we did, even though I only had my summer shoes on.

GEORGIOU: Get the bread, Lena.

LENA: We lost her in the crowds and our daddy doesn't know where we are. But it'll be all right because we have a secret signal so we can find each other if we ever get lost.

OMAR: What is it?

LENA: We have to hoot like an owl.

OMAR: Our father was in the old army. He was taken away – we don't know where he went and then soldiers took our house. We let Elena out so they wouldn't eat her.

LENA: Who's Elena?

OMAR: Our chicken.

LENA: Go and call now, Georgiou.

GEORGIOU: Is it time?

LENA: Daddy will have fed the horses and he'll be drinking his coffee now …

(Georgiou climbs up into the open arch of the tower. He puts his hands to his mouth and makes a call, like an owl.)

SCENE 6

(The Fortune Teller sits on his wagon, a mug of coffee in his hand and the parrot perched beside him.)

(sound effect: an owl hooting)

FORTUNE TELLER: Hear that, Lucky? Every time I hear an owl, I think it might be them.

(He puts his hands to his mouth and calls back.)

SCENE 7

(Fran is sitting at a table in her house studying a piece of paper. Bruno comes in with some parcels.)

FRAN: What did you get me, Bruno?

BRUNO: The market's almost empty, Mrs Sorkiny – I had to queue for two hours for a few carrots and some black bread.

FRAN: Bruno, can you read this for me? I haven't got my glasses.

BRUNO: Doesn't say much. It's a kid's drawing – of a dog.

FRAN: A dog?

BRUNO: Says, "Here's a dog for you madam like you had when you were little."

FRAN: *(astonished)* That boy on the train – he drew me a dog?

BRUNO: It's got some writing on the back – says,
"Isabella Sorkiny – 15 Rue Bel Tesoro …"

FRAN: *(grabbing the paper)* Sorkiny? But that's my name …

BRUNO: Must be a thousand Sorkinys in this city alone …

FRAN: I have two daughters – I haven't seen them for
many years … We argued, they went away …

BRUNO: It's a common name.

FRAN: Of course – except – the boy, he said his mother, she used to sing the lullaby …

BRUNO: All mothers sing lullabies, Mrs Sorkiny.

FRAN: You're right – except – what if they were mine, my grandchildren, and they're out there … all alone?

SCENE 8

(At the church tower Georgiou is packing up as Omar goes through his bag desperately.)

SASHA: I told you to be careful and now you've lost Auntie's address!

OMAR: *(nearly crying)* I drew a picture on the train, I must have done it on the wrong piece of paper …

SASHA: I can't trust you for a minute!

OMAR: I can remember it, Rue Bel Tesoro.

SASHA: Are you sure? *(to Georgiou)* Do you know where that is – Rue Bel Tesoro?

GEORGIOU: I might do.

SASHA: Take us there.

GEORGIOU: All right then, but I want the dog.

OMAR: No!

GEORGIOU: You expect me to take you there for nothing?

OMAR: You can't give him Valentine!

LENA: I don't think we should take his doggie.

GEORGIOU: What do you know about it? You know how to get us money? Get us food?

OMAR: Sasha!

SASHA: *(to Georgiou)* Take us there and you can have the dog.

(Everyone stares at her, horrified.)

SCENE 9

(Norma is skipping and singing to herself in the Rue Bel Tesoro. Fran appears looking at the ruins of the houses.)

FRAN: You girl, you know the Sorkinys?

(Norma stares at her.)

FRAN: Where do the Sorkinys live?

NORMA: Everyone's gone.

FRAN: *(calling towards the ruined houses)* Isabella! Alicia! It's me! Mama!

NORMA: Cats live in the houses now.

FRAN: I met two children. They had my name, but I didn't know that. They might have been my relatives … *(remembering)* "a treasure slipping through my fingers". Blind, blind, too stupid to live – I live to find my family and I didn't know them when they came! I only have a pass for one day. I must go back. You want to earn some money?

NORMA: Yes I do!

FRAN: Then listen very carefully …

SCENE 10

(Omar and Sasha stand with Georgiou and Lena and their pram in an alleyway.)

OMAR: This isn't the right place. This place is all bombed.

GEORGIOU: This is it. So hand over the dog.

SASHA: You heard him, Omar.

OMAR: No!

LENA: I don't want to eat the doggie.

GEORGIOU: Be quiet, Lena, and do as you're told.

OMAR: You give him Valentine and you're a murderer!

LENA: Daddy would never take somebody's dog.

GEORGIOU: Daddy isn't here, is he?

(Lena starts to cry.)

GEORGIOU: We can sell it, they're eating rats in the city …

OMAR: Please, Sasha …

GEORGIOU: *(to Lena)* Do you want to find our food? Do you want to get us money and find us places to sleep at night?

OMAR: Run, Valentine, run! Run!

(They all look at the pram. Nothing happens.)

LENA: If you take their dog then you're just as bad as the soldiers.

(Georgiou reaches into his rucksack, takes out one of the apples in a bottle.)

GEORGIOU: *(angry)* All right then, take this, earn your own living, I'm going. It's not my job to look after you.

(Georgiou goes. Omar and Sasha stand shocked.)

LENA: *(calling after him)* Georgiou!

(The children look at the devastated street.)

SASHA: There's no one here, Omar. All the families are gone.

OMAR: We'll find ours, we'll get Valentine to sniff Mummy's jumper and follow the scent like a tracker dog.

SASHA: Valentine can't track, he never even gets out of that pram.

OMAR: We *will* find Mummy, we'll just have to look harder.

SASHA: We have no food and no money and no one to look after us. How can we keep on looking?

(Omar sits down in the rubble.)

OMAR: I want to go home.

SASHA: We can't go home. Other people live in our house now.

(Norma arrives.)

NORMA: What's your name?

SASHA: What's it to you?

NORMA: I've got a delivery but you've got to show me papers like at a roadblock.

OMAR: A delivery – for us?

SASHA: It's a story, Omar, she's making it up.

(Omar gets out his papers anyway and Norma looks at them.
She walks away, then comes back – with a suitcase.
The children stare at it.)

NORMA: A grandma left it – for you.

(Norma puts down the case and runs off.)

OMAR: *(looking at a note stuck to it)* There's a letter …

(He hands it to Sasha.)

SASHA: *(reads)* My children, if you should find this letter, know that I'm sorry for not helping you when I might have. I'm sorry for so much more than this, but leave you a present – to help you now. Come to me, at the address I have written here. It doesn't matter if you're my grandchildren or if we simply share the same name. All children are precious, let me say this to you when I never thought to say it to my own daughters. And bring your little dog. Yours, Francesca Sorkiny.

(Omar opens the suitcase.)

OMAR: Teeth!

SASHA: We can trade these, for food.

OMAR: We're rich! We can go and find her. We can sneak through the barbed wire and go back. She left us her business. She loves us.

(Georgiou arrives back.)

GEORGIOU: *(to Lena)* So, you going to sit there all day then or what?

LENA: Georgiou!

GEORGIOU: *(smiling)* Come on.

OMAR: We're going back, to find our grandmother. You could come with us, if you like.

GEORGIOU: We're all right on our own.

LENA: Let's go with them, Georgiou. I'm tired of being all alone.

GEORGIOU: It's my job to get us back to Father.

LENA: You can call him. Then we'll just start walking, and we'll keep calling until he hears us.

(Georgiou looks at the others, then he puts his hands to his mouth and calls like an owl. The children start to walk.)

OMAR: How do you get the apple in the bottle?

GEORGIOU: *(to Lena)* Shall we tell him?

OMAR: I'll keep it a secret forever,
I promise …

GEORGIOU: Well, it's like this …

*(sound effect: an
owl hooting)*

A map

Fran's house

church tower

Fortune Teller's wagon

RUE BEL TESORO

train station

Ideas for guided reading

Learning objectives: develop a range of personal strategies for learning new and irregular words; deduce characters' reasons for behaviour from their actions; offer reasons and evidence for views; identify how talk varies with age, familiarity, gender and purpose; create roles showing how behaviour can be interpreted from different viewpoints

Curriculum links: History: What was it like for children in the Second World War?

Citizenship: Children's rights – human rights

Interest words: chaos, unmoved, furiously poison, business, whistle, mysteries, roadblocks, barricades, horrified, treasure, rucksack, rubble

Resources: coloured pens, paper, simple props for performance

Getting started

This book can be read over two or more guided reading sessions.

- Encourage children to look at the front cover and to discuss what kind of story this is.

- Ask a child to read the blurb aloud and explain that the book is a play about two children looking for their family during a war.

- Ask children where and when they think the play is set. What evidence do they have?

- Turn to p2. Read the characters' names and ask children to predict what might happen to them in the play.

Reading and responding

- Decide who in the group will read each part. Discuss how to make a voice sound old or young and explain how voices vary with the mood of the speaker and who they are talking to, e.g. *How are you going to make Fran sound really cross?*

- Ask children to read the first two scenes together in their chosen parts.